WILDER WINDS

Bel Olid is a writer and translator and has published a number of books, both in original Catalan and in translation from English, Italian, German and French. Bel Olid has won numerous prizes and awards including the Premi QWERTY, Premi Documenta and Premi Roc Boronat. From 2015 they have been president of the Associació d'Escriptors en Llengua Catalana and, from 2013 to 2015, president of the European Council of Literary Translators' Associations. They currently live in Badalona.

Laura McGloughlin has been a freelance translator from Catalan and Spanish since completing a master's degree in literary translation at the University of East Anglia. She was awarded the inaugural British Centre for Literary Translation Catalan-English Translation Mentorship in 2011. Among other works she has translated work by Llüisa Cunillé, Maria Barbal, Flavia Company, Toni Hill Gumbao, and Joan Brossa.

'Beneath their calm surface, Bel Olid's lucid tales seethe with potential violence; moments of quiet charm alternate, in Laura McGloughlin's deft translation, with glimpses of the dangerous precariousness of women's lives.'
—Shaun Whiteside

'Bel Olid tells you the most terrible things in the most beautiful way.'
—Marta Rojals

'Charming and comforting on the one hand; like a vast abyss of violence and danger, it is stimulating and disturbing on the other.'
—Júlia Sentís, *Núvol*

'Simple, everyday descriptions transport the reader to places and moments, producing sensations that we can all relate to ... an excellent read.'
—*Nosaltresllegim.cat*

FUM D'ESTAMPA PRESS

www.fumdestampa.com

This translation has been published in Great Britain
by Fum d'Estampa Press Limited 2022

001

Original Catalan title: *Vents més salvatges*
Text copyright ©Bel Olid, 2016
Original edition published by Empúries
Edition published by arrangement with Asterisc Agents.
All rights reserved

English language translation © Laura McGloughlin, 2022

The moral rights of the author and translator have been asserted
Set in Minion Pro

Printed and bound by TJ Books Ltd, Padstow, Cornwall
A CIP catalogue record for this book is available from the British Library

ISBN: 978-1-913744-03-8

This work was translated with the help of a grant from the Institut Ramon Llull.

institut
ramon llull
Catalan Language and Culture

WILDER WINDS

BEL OLID

Translated by

LAURA MCGLOUGHLIN

CONTENTS

I am in need of music that would flow
Over my fretful, feeling fingertips,
Over my bitter-tainted, trembling lips,
With melody, deep, clear, and liquid-slow.
ELIZABETH BISHOP

To Sarah: sea, wind, home.

SHE'S A WOMAN

Helena, the masters' daughter, had invited me to play with her. Actually, it wasn't so much that Helena had invited me as she had found me there, sitting in her dining room. Stiff as a board, intimidated by the modern and luxurious ambience of the house, I gulped at the glass of milk the *senyora* had offered me before leaving me on my own.

My aunt had asked the masters if I could stay with her in the help's room for a couple of days until my mother was better. At that time my mother was in and out of hospital a lot, so I spent many hours alone at home, and someone must have realised that a girl of my age, almost a young woman, shouldn't be alone so much. Aunt worked in the masters' house and slept in a little room that, while not very big, was well-furnished. It had a queen-size bed, a mirrored wardrobe and a window with carnations.

Aunt was in the kitchen scrubbing something when the *senyora* had told her to give me a glass of milk — *for the love of God, girls this age need to grow* — and then made me sit in the dining room. I sat there, knees close together and hands folded on my lap, one on top of the other, as my mother had taught me young ladies do.

Helena came with a sheaf of cut-out paper dolls and some scissors and sat opposite me. She offered me a sheet with a little girl who was surrounded by clothes and accessories drawn on it and devoted herself to watching me as I cut out skirts, shoes and hats. From time to time she asked obvious questions, as if to break the silence, and I didn't know whether to answer or not. Then she came closer, leaning over the table, almost climbing onto it, to pick up the cut-out doll and put a yellow dress on her and her breath, so close, smelled of fruit. I remember how red my face turned as I thought of my aunt in the kitchen, perhaps coming in any minute, and I got up abruptly.

'I'm going to the toilet,' I mumbled, and opened the first door I found in the hallway.

Perhaps I was already flustered by the time I got to the bathroom, or perhaps she was such a vibrant and spirited contrast to my dry, sick, elderly mother, but I was struck by the image of the splendid woman before the mirror, arms up, no t-shirt, no bra, nothing more than smooth skin and a double-edge razor in her right hand, halfway through shaving her left armpit.

She didn't flinch, but just smiled and said she'd be finished in a minute, and that there was another bathroom at the end of the hallway. Those eyes looked at me as intently as those of her daughter, and that skin seemed so smooth. I didn't move, and she continued to look at me. Then I heard Helena's voice — *aren't you coming?* — and closed the door behind me. I ran to the end of the hallway, opened another door, and sat in the dark for a long time to let my breath return to normal, summoning up all the courage I had to go back to the dining room.

Then Aunt knocked on the door and told me the hospital had called and she had to go, that the masters were going out that night, and that I should behave and not annoy Helena.

When they went out — the *senyora* in a dress like the ones in the movies, the *senyor* in a tie and shiny shoes — Helena dragged me to her bedroom.

'We can't go to the concert with them, but we'll put on the record,' she said.

I heard the nasal voices and the catchy tunes for the first time and, used as I was to boleros and folk songs, I didn't know whether I liked it or not, but I felt privileged to be there, dancing in Helena's room.

That night I danced with my pyjama top rolled up, my ponytail undone and my cheeks burning. When we'd played the record a thousand times and it was late and time to go to sleep, Helena said I could stay with her, breath like fruit and skin like silk, but I said thank you, and instead ran to Aunt's ample bed.

All night I gazed at the carnations, a tickling like ants running around my insides.

My Aunt arrived in the small hours of the morning, her face grey. She would hang on a little while yet, my mother, and Aunt's hospital runs followed one after the other as the days went by. I stayed at the masters' house: the *senyora* insisted. But I never again surprised her half-naked.

Since then I've always knocked on doors before daring to open them, since then I've always entered the bathrooms of unfamiliar houses both nervous and hopeful. Since then I've always been fascinated by my own undressed image in the mirror when I shave my armpits. Since then that music has always had the scent of fruit, of skin like silk, of pending death in the background.

STATIC

There shouldn't be so much traffic; it's not even rush hour. She notices she's tapping the steering wheel, silent regular beats, and stops. Is she nervous because she's nervous or because of the unmoving traffic? She's late, as usual. Her mother will be livid, as usual. So what?

She turns on the radio in the hope her favourite song is being played at this very moment as a sign of goodwill from the universe — *I'm worried about you, Sara. I want you to be alright. I'll treat you well.* The universe as a precarious substitute for a god in which she couldn't believe. The universe as the tender and loving mother she'd like to have had.

Guys talking about economics again, no music. Maybe the universe wants to make things a little more difficult for her. You can't expect things to happen just like that; you have to work at it a bit. She turns the tuning dial, the cars begin to move, and the white noise of nothingness accompanies her for a while. It's an old car with an old radio and she likes being able to listen to static noise if she pleases.

When she was small, she used to sit with her youngest brother Toni in front of the TV and watch the grey, white and black screen that meant it wasn't tuned in to any channel. Someone (Anna, the eldest, or Uri the middle child, sometimes their father, normally their mother) would always find them there and put on cartoons. They wouldn't complain; they liked Tom and Jerry, too. But after a while, if they were left alone, Sara would turn the dial, Toni would smile, and they'd be happy a little while longer.

They can't do that anymore. The screen turns blue: a solid, perfect blue offering no escape and allowing nothing to be read between the lines that isn't aseptic, boring blue. There's no blue noise instead of white noise, either; just silence. For that reason, she doesn't have a TV.

Toni will be there today. Everyone will be there. Her mother will criticise Sara's dress or say she's wearing too much make-up or none at all, and Anna will offer her a lipstick. Uri will say she's a grown-up, leave her the hell alone. Toni won't say anything, but will wink at her when no-one's looking.

It's her mother's birthday but she doesn't want to go. She wouldn't mind if the traffic jam lasted forever. She'd be there, sitting in her old car, listening to the nothingness on the old radio. Pretending she's going somewhere, that being late again isn't her fault. Sitting there, without a guilty conscience for doing nothing, following the car in front, stopping and starting, stopping and starting.

And then she's arrived and found parking just in front of her mother's house, as if the universe were apparently nudging her in the nicest way. Sara rings the bell and realises she's left the present in the car. It's not as if her mother would have liked it, anyway.

Her nephew, Anna's son, opens the door.

'It's Auntie Sara!' he shouts and jumps up around her neck.

She hugs him and enters the house with the boy on her neck, the living weight in her arms, her nephew's head nestling into her shoulder. She stands still for a moment, not moving, just breathing, inhaling the little boy smell of strawberry mixed with traces of shit (he must have been outside playing with the dog) and feels she is exactly where she should be.

Her mother is in the kitchen, dishing up the second course. Anna and Uri are fighting about something, definitely politics. Toni is reading her younger niece, Lola, a book they'd liked a lot as children. And Pau is still on her neck, for too long now. And the white noise of happiness surrounds everything, even if only for a moment.

They had told her very clearly what the camp was like: the line of containers serving as houses; the sun beating down on it all; the dust; the communal tap at the entrance. Officially, it wasn't called a 'camp' as 'camp' is an ugly word that brings to mind concentration, refugees and the military. Officially, it was called an 'open centre', an improvement on the 'internment centre' which was also called a 'centre' but was really a prison.

Margie knew because they had told her what the camp was like and she knew not to expect much of it. But deep down she thought an open centre had to be quite a lot better than an internment centre. She'd never gone to the internment centre either, but she imagined it to be like the prisons in films, with grills and barred doors that close behind you. Clean, sterile. The residents (the prisoners, really) in neat uniforms, each of them in their cell, and grey dominating everything, like a still winter sea that imparts a sad calm, but a calm nonetheless.

Perhaps it was because she'd got the idea in her head that the camp would be 'something better' than a prison that it shocked her so much the day she walked into it for the first time. Aunt Claire came to get her one Wednesday at the end of summer, and during the car journey she told her that a group from Syria had arrived a couple of weeks before and that people had sent food, clothes and toys. Those fleeing war are always better received than those trying to escape poverty, especially if the poverty is in a black skin, as if poverty isn't a bomb that will end up killing you.

Margie said nothing en route to the camp but nodded along to her aunt's chatter and looked out the window at how the landscape was emptying of houses and filling with solar panels, half-collapsed walls, dust. To a stranger's eyes, the colour of the island's landscape in the summer might seem implausibly monotonous: the stone-coloured buildings; the sand-coloured stone; the sand the colour of the dry vegetation clinging on with all its might.

Margie, however, liked the fact that there was little varia-
tion between one element and another, the infinite gamut of
yellows, beiges, browns. She liked the way the hues of the island
matched the blondish chestnut of her hair. When she looked
in the mirror, she imagined her dark blue eyes to be the sea
surrounding everything.

'Nearly there,' said her aunt. 'Here on the left is the internment
centre, and a little further on we turn right and we'll be there.'

She should have taken that large, ugly, half-falling down
building as a warning sign: this was not a clean prison like in
the movies, this was four infinite walls barely providing shelter
against the weather. It was surely dirty inside, and mosquitos,
ants and bugs must have got in. It certainly looked nothing like
the sterile prisons in the television series.

She thought all this but continued to hope the camp would
be better. There were children in the camp, and they must surely
live in appropriate conditions. People had donated clothes and
toys and so there must be some sort of room for them to go and
play in, and in the evening children have to bathe before going
to bed. In the evening the camp must smell of baby lotion, baby
food and warm milk. Like her house when Jude was born.

At the roundabout, just before turning, she saw a group
waiting for the bus. Three or four women with children in prams
were talking among themselves in dresses that were once brightly
coloured. There were also six or seven men with old trousers,
old t-shirts, old eyes.

'Let's park here, ok? Now when we get out, let me talk. In
theory you shouldn't be able to come in here because you're
a minor, but the new person in charge is very nice and I've
already told her that my niece would be coming today to give
me a hand. If she asks whether you're a volunteer with the
association, you just say: "yes".'

They each took a box from the car boot, went through the

open gate, and poked their heads into the office. Margie automatically followed Claire as if her legs weren't her own, as if the arms holding the box weren't hers, as if it were impossible that the body penetrating that underworld of hot air was hers.

'Hey Claire, what have you brought? What are you carrying? Your niece is pretty, looks like her aunt.'

The woman winked and Claire smiled, put the box on the floor, and indicated to Margie that she should do the same.

'Margie, we have to sort out some paperwork. You can take a walk around.'

'You can't take photos, or enter the apartments or bother anyone. Ok, sweetheart? If anything happens, I'm screwed.'

She didn't want to in the least, but she left the office. Out of the corner of her eye she looked at the open gate, quashed her desire to flee and wait in the car, took a deep breath, looked around and started walking.

Her aunt and the other volunteers had told her very clearly what the camp was like: the line of containers serving as houses, the sun beating down on it all, the dust, the communal tap at the entrance. She could point out every element and say that yes, they'd told her the truth, the containers and sun and dust and tap were there. And at the same time, she wanted to say that: no, this couldn't be it.

They hadn't told her about the stage-like cement platforms where the dwellings were placed, as if life there was a theatrical performance that no-one was watching because it hurt to see. They hadn't told her about the brutal lack of trees and the complete lack of any shade beyond that made by the containers or the bunks the men had dragged outside because it was so suffocating that it was impossible to be inside. There were little plaques on the top left of each container, placed on the hardest surface of the corrugated steel, ten by fifteen centimetres, with the serial number and a European Union flag. An insult, a joke.

Everything they had told her about was there and yet they

hadn't told her about the dirty-faced children, the flies hunting their snot, and their gazes accustomed to seeing only cement and more cement, metal and more metal, dust and more dust. The tired mothers, the bored old folk, the men outside all day standing at the point on the motorway where a truck seeking to take them away as day labourers would pass, sometimes for a few hours' work, sometimes for a few days. If they hadn't got lucky, the men came back even more humiliated, even more worn out, even more trapped.

They hadn't told her any of this because they had seen it all so many times that it being any other way didn't seem possible, and for the volunteers, for Claire, the word 'camp' naturally included 'refugee' and 'concentration'. Some had been there for years, some had seen their children born there. Like the volunteers, some began to think it couldn't be any other way. They didn't leave through the gate which was always open during the day.

'Hello.'

The girl, a little younger than Margie, came over to her and smiled at her in a way that seemed impossibly easy. She walked beside her, asked her what she was doing there and looked at her with her big eyes, the blue of a paler sea.

'Come on, we'll go behind here, it's better there.'

At the end of the fifth row of containers, between the platforms and the wire fence that separated the camp from an enormous empty plot, was a prickly pear tree with ripe fruit, intensely orange with threatening thorns. The girl took a knife from her pocket, picked a couple of pears, skilfully peeled them and offered Margie her open, dripping palm. She seemed immune to the thorns.

'My name is Maimunà. And yours?'

Margie ate prickly pears for the first time that afternoon. She listened to Maimunà's fluent English, the story of her journey, the days that became weeks that became months in the camp; almost two years already. The damp cold that entered her bones in the winter, the uselessness of covering herself with a thousand blankets. The sticky heat in the summer, the poor refuge from the sun that was the hard shadow of the containers.

'Margie, we have to go. Maimunà, how are things? I knew you two would get on.'

Maimunà smiled, hugged Margie, kissed her on the cheek and whispered, 'Will you come back?' Such tenderness seemed out of place to her in the setting of cement and dust offered by the camp.

That week was hard for Margie. While she ate dinner with her parents and Jude, with every spoonful she was thinking: *I am here and they are there.* In bed, between clean sheets. In the shower. While she watched TV, while she read. *I am here and they are there.* And then, like an echo, the kiss on the cheek: 'Will you come back?'

The weekend was the hardest. She'd met up with her friends, Keith with eyes like a clear sea, Nadja's easy smile. *I am here and they are there.* She is there.

Though she only thought it every so often and less and less frequently, she sensed it would never leave her. That phrase like a jar of cold water, treacherous as a dagger: *I am here and they are there.* It came to her at unexpected moments. Eating a chocolate ice-cream, trying on a dress, going to the market. *I am here and they are there.* 'Will you come back?'

Partly to overcome this endless feeling, and partly to see Maimunà again, she asked Aunt Claire if she could become a volunteer. She wanted to help in some way. When school started, she blocked out her Saturdays: she'd go to the camp with a group of young volunteers and they'd organise games for the youngest. She'd meet Maimunà and they'd chat. Margie remembered her life before, her life the previous spring, and it seemed happily naive; internment centres that were well-kept prisons, open centres that weren't camps.

Between school and the centre, the last term before university was intense. That year, summer arrived almost by surprise, a shedding of layers of clothing, barely noticeable, until one morning only a strappy dress over underwear scented with fabric softener remained. On June 23rd Margie turned eighteen and, perhaps by accident or perhaps because Claire wanted to give her a present, a show had been planned at the Peace Laboratory beside the camp.

Lots of people were taking part: an Italian singer was coming, five poets from the island, an Algerian playwright and a Belgian theatre company. The audience would be the refugees from the camp, those who lived in the laboratory huts, the volunteers, even some press. It would be a lovely night, or so they hoped.

The Peace Lab was a halfway house. When the refugees found some sort of more or less stable work, they left the camp. Later, when they inevitably lost that work through some absurd law, they couldn't come back. So, Friar Dionysius would welcome them in some broken-down huts that were very close to the internment and open centres, but with trees, a dozen chickens and some goats in precarious enclosures. There was an open-air amphitheatre, an imitation of those of ancient Greece dating from when the friar's brother was president and there was plenty to go around. But that was a long time ago. Later, the government's revenge had been to let it fall apart in the desire that all hope there might die.

All in all, there were so many people who needed that corner of feigned peace that, despite the friar's advanced age and the difficulties of maintenance, the Laboratory remained open, as stubborn as a weed rooted in Malta's dry earth. On one wall, amidst 80s magazine covers, a plaque commemorated illustrious collaborators. Kennedy, Mandela, island celebrities.

As she organised the drinks and sandwiches on the table serving as a bar, to the left of the stalls, Margie was thinking about the brand new moped her parents had given her that morning. The joy on her father's face, her mother warning her not to go out without a helmet, Jude asking to tag along on her first spin. Margie was happy until, mingled with the happiness, the jar of cold water: *I am here and they are there, and now I can go where I like and they will be there. She will be there.*

She'd gone to the Laboratory on the moped, of course. It had been hard to leave Jude at home: 'I have lots to do, it's not for kids, you can come another day. If you like, we'll go for a spin tomorrow.' It was a brand new Vespa, a shiny cream colour a little lighter than the stones of the island, and a little lighter than her hair. A new Vespa, but retro, with a chocolate-coloured leather seat and mirrors either side. Two wheels that would give her more freedom. *I am here and they are there.*

'Margie sweetheart, I'll stay here, you go and watch the show.'

She sat in the last row and waited for the others to get there. The sun was setting. Someone lit a path of candles leading to the stalls and people started to arrive. They had dressed up however they could with what they had. The women wore make-up, the men had changed their t-shirts for shirts and the children opened their eyes wide; many couldn't remember ever being in such a beautiful place.

Margie felt a hand on her shoulder, Maimunà was sitting down beside her. She was wearing a floral blouse, short jeans and red sandals that Margie had outgrown and given to her.

'Look, I'm wearing lipstick,' she told her and Margie felt a tingle in her sex and thought she must be like Aunt Claire, whom her parents secretly criticised.

The show began: the songs, the poems, a slightly absurd play they didn't really understand but that spoke of the sea.

'The last time I saw the sea was when I arrived in the dinghy. I was so exhausted I don't remember what colour your sea is,' said Maimunà. There was no trace of drama, she was saying a truth out loud and that was that.

Margie felt Maimunà's hand close to hers, Maimunà's breath close to hers, and the keys of the moped in her pocket.

'Come on,' she said. And they left.

Discreetly, without anyone noticing, not thinking too much, not wanting to remember that tomorrow existed, they got on the moped, took the Wied Iz-Żurrieq road, and arrived at the sea. It was night and there was a full moon. The water was dark and warm, like a cave, like a uterus, like the desire sharpening their fragile happiness.

That night, swimming nude in front of Filfla island, her dark eyes gazing into Maimunà's pale eyes, the spell of the jar of cold water was undone. I am here and she is too, she thought.

ANNA, ANNE, ANNA

There are memories that shine like a brand new coin on the pavement when touched by the midday sun and you, walking with your head bowed, looking at the ground, wake up suddenly, pick it up and feel you are very lucky. Then you look ahead, the coin in your pocket, and don't yet dare spend it. You do nothing with it, but for days you come across it whenever you put your hand in your jacket pocket and it's as if the sun momentarily dazzles you again.

We were going home from the tobacconist's. We often went there, though no-one at home smoked. We'd buy matches, magazines, pencils, sweets, sports newspapers. That day I went with my mother who hadn't wanted to buy me a book. Things were tight at home and I knew I shouldn't ask for things twice. I often didn't even ask for things once, and perhaps that day I didn't say anything about the book but simply thought I'd like to read a *Famous Five*, or *Tintin*. I don't really remember. I didn't like those books much, but they were the only ones available in the tobacconist's.

I was going home with my mother, looking at the ground a couple of steps behind her, and didn't come across any coin. Instead, I found a book, open on the ground. I picked it up and looked around, afraid someone might turn around looking for it. 'There's a book,' I said softly, as if I wished to inform the potential owner, probably a woman. I didn't know any men who read at that time, and the boys in school only did so reluctantly. It seemed to me that books always belonged to women. Men wrote them and women read them. I truly believed this, so much so that it was years before I discovered that Enid Blyton was a woman's name. But that's another story, another coin I'll spend another day.

'There's a book,' I said softly and, as no owner appeared, I adopted it. Now it was mine, it was my book, and I shook it clean as best I could. The cover and some pages, especially from the beginning, were missing. It was unglued, but mostly in order, and I started reading it:

'I had to stop yesterday, though I was nowhere near finished. I'm dying to tell you about another one of our clashes, but before I do, I'd like to say this…'

'You idiot!' my mother shouted at me.

I closed my eyes and covered my face with the book, but the smack never came. Only a little slap on the head, almost affectionate. My poor mother had arrived home not realising I'd been dawdling, lost among the pages, and had been scared.

'There's a book,' I repeated, a little louder. And she let me keep it and I loved her for it. My hand, still shining like a coin in the sun, was in my mother's all the way home, the book gripped in the other.

'North Amsterdam was very heavily bombed on Sunday. There was apparently a great deal of destruction. Entire streets are in ruins, and it will take a while for them to dig out all the bodies. So far there have been two hundred dead and countless wounded; the hospitals are bursting at the seams. We've been told of children searching forlornly in the smouldering ruins for their dead parents.'

I read until dinnertime and, when they made me go to bed, I continued to read under the sheets with a small torch they bought me for when I went to camp, just as we've all done. I read until there were no more pages and mourned all that had been written that I couldn't read, because instead of a book it was a piece of a book, unglued pages and no cover. I felt bad leaving her there, alone in that attic, not knowing what would become of her.

At the top of half of the pages, it said *The Diary of Anne Frank* and on the other half 'Anne Frank', and I realised that Anne was a girl's name, that it was my aunt's name, my cousin's name, it was a girl's name like mine. And this Anne had written this book, and suddenly it seemed possible. It seemed that someday, lost on some street, there might be a book with my name at the top and a girl who might find it. Or maybe even a boy.

The next day, as I was eating breakfast, I told my mother the story. 'That book is for adults,' she said. 'Don't read it anymore.' And I said nothing and put it in my schoolbag.

I carried it everywhere for a long time, that book. I re-read it in secret — *that book is for adults* — and imagined a different ending every time, different scenes for every page that was missing.

For my communion I was given lots of diaries. Everyone who felt they had to give me a present and couldn't stretch too far went for the cheap option — *let's give her a diary, she's very studious, she'll surely like to write down her stuff.*

I accumulated seven or eight: white, with sky blue or pink drawings of doves and angels, gilt-edged paper, with padlocks with interchangeable keys. *Dear Diary*, it said on the cover. And I wondered whether Anne Frank had written her book in this kind of notebook, whether she too had carefully hidden the keys in nooks around the house.

I don't know what I wrote in them, or what happened to them. They must have been tossed out during one of mother's untimely spring cleans. One day the book wasn't there either. I didn't dare ask.

'*...I keep trying to find a way to become what I'd like to be and what I could be if...if only there were no other people in the world.*'

Later, when I discovered libraries, when I was grown up and I could buy myself all the books I wanted to read, I could have searched for that *Diary of Anne Frank*. I could have read it from start to finish.

But I preferred not to. There are memories that shine like a brand-new coin on the pavement when touched by the midday sun and you, walking with your head bowed and looking at the ground, wake up suddenly, pick it up and feel you are very lucky. That, I still carry in my pocket.

One of the moments of the day Luba Kashmir liked best was the time she spent lazing in the mornings before getting up. She usually woke up around seven, but never got up before eight. She would allow her body to awaken little by little; stretch her toes, wiggle her ears, take time opening her eyes. She never closed her curtains and if it wasn't winter, a friendly brightness filtered through the window.

In front of the bed, Baba Luba had a heavy solid wood shelf that had been in the dining room years before. She had moved it into her room because on waking she liked to look at the forty-two dolls her son had brought back for her over the years he'd worked as a sailor on whatever ship might want to take him. They were cheap dolls in poor taste, adorned with the traditional costumes of remote countries. Those dolls kept Baba Luba company, which is why she had asked the boy on the second floor and his friend to bring the shelf into her room. On opening her eyes in the morning, she looked at them and a flush would rise to her cheeks.

She never got up before eight, but never later than half past, and in a nightshirt and thick shawl she would go to the kitchen and prepare a cup of watery coffee, take a pickled cucumber from the glass jar, and spread butter on a slice of bread. She would listen to the radio in the morning, Baba Luba, while she rinsed the dishes from breakfast, washed her armpits with cold water, put her hair up in a bun and got dressed.

They hadn't always called her Baba Luba in the district. The neighbours used to call her Lubishka as a little girl. Luba the Beauty, the boys would call her, before she married. For a few years, before becoming a mother, she was simply Luba. But she was so old that by now there was no-one who remembered a time when she wasn't Baba Luba, no grandchildren but still Baba Luba, because such an old woman simply must call herself granny.

She lived alone and contented, cradled in her daily routine. If she thought about it, it would seem strange, that 'daily routine'. She had lived through a lot, Baba Luba. Changes of regime, laws, currency. Inflation, poverty upon poverty. She had lived through a lot, and it could feel as if life never repeated itself at all: rather every few years everything just turned upside down. But for a long time now, since Taras' death, when the double bed felt empty and she no longer had to get up with her husband to prepare his breakfast, she would repeat almost the exact same actions every day, finding a kind of steadying homeland in this repetition.

Life had taught her that stability wasn't to be found outside on the streets. That as soon as you get used to how others live, everything changes. Daily actions, the simpler the better, were easier to maintain, and she lived contentedly, if not happily, following her little rituals. Waking up little by little, looking at her dolls. Breakfasting on whatever was there, coffee with a slice of bread if there was any. Listening to the radio while she rinsed the dishes and washed herself. Obstinately going over the map of her small homeland formed of attainable habits.

After lunch on that icy winter day, Baba Luba went downstairs to see her neighbour for a while. It was Saturday and her neighbour had her granddaughter there. The girl had switched on the television, the volume low so they wouldn't be disturbed by the voice raised in anger. The speaker was talking about the protests in Independence Square, people of all ages coming out, the government that would have to give in sooner or later. President Yanukovych was on the television, pleading for calm, praising the work of the Berkut, asking for common sense from the good citizens — *be sensible, don't leave your homes.*

The neighbour's granddaughter pulled up her sweater and showed them her back. It was a landscape of blues and reds, of tensed, injured, inflamed skin. She pointed at the table where there was a foreign newspaper open on the international section.

'It was them. And I was lucky, they say there were deaths.'

In the photograph was a row of men in helmets, with shields, body armour and steely gazes. A row of seemingly unmoving men, not even a centimetre, truncheons in their hands, weapons at their waists. And people screaming, raising their hands, and that was what had happened in the square.

'They should hang their heads in shame, those scoundrels in uniform. Child, get dressed, don't get cold, the stove doesn't work well,' said her neighbour as she handed her granddaughter some sweets that were just like the ones she liked to eat when she was a little girl.

Baba Luba was uneasy in her chair and looked away from the newspaper and informed them that it was time for her to go home. There was only one floor between her neighbour's on the third to her home on the fourth, but the images of the injured back, the President in a suit and tie, the police with gazes so hard they didn't seem human, were etched onto her retinas. The images were carved into her mind and weighed so heavily on her that it was difficult to make her way upstairs.

She didn't sleep well the following nights, Baba Luba. Like every day, she repeated her actions, looked at her dolls, made herself coffee and rinsed the dishes. But she didn't find the comfort in them she had found before. The images came back to her and she was expelled from her little daily homeland, she wasn't cradled by the tranquillity of her routine.

As she washed before the mirror, she was surprised by her sad face, swollen eyelids, the turned-down corners of her mouth. The perfect bun that no longer contributed to the serenity she'd grown fond of over the years.

'This is what I've become — a sad old woman.'

The words echoed against the tiled walls of the bathroom. Then the silence became more present than ever, and all the accumulated solitude fell on her as if no longer her friend. She was there for a long while, Baba Luba, looking at herself in the mirror, until she decided to take it down.

It was a cheap mirror, forty centimetres by fifty, which the boy on the second floor and his friend had hung when the one she'd had all her life had chipped. It was fixed to the wall with a couple of hooks, and it wasn't too hard for her to remove it. Going down the four floors weighed down by the mirror and walking the twenty minutes to Independence Square, encumbered by her overcoat and gloves, was another thing altogether.

Despite the cold, she reached the square with her cheeks burning. There was a crowd, and it seemed very young. Determined, she turned to the line of policemen, the multitude opening like a stupefied sea to allow through the old lady lugging a mirror under her arm.

Reaching the end, before the impassive barrier of the Berkut, she raised the mirror and turned it so the policeman could see himself, his clenched teeth, his eyes of steel. The policeman's blank stare focused on the reflection, his expression changed for a moment and he made as if to say something.

'This is what you've become, son,' said Baba Luba.

And then an elbow from a colleague called the policeman to order, once again the blank stare, once again the return to the anonymity of the row.

Someone started clapping beside Baba Luba and the clapping extended throughout the square, people clapped their hands through thick gloves and waves of curiosity not knowing why they were clapping. There was only the feeling that something worthy of clapping for had happened, and they felt the warmth pass from one to another.

She came home alone that day, Baba Luba. Slowly, with the fatigue of the years weighing on her, sitting down on some corner or other from time to time in order to gather strength. She looked at herself then, and saw her white hair under a crimson scarf, her shining eyes, her happiness. 'I'm not a sad old woman,' she said to herself, proudly. And so, thanks to an out of the ordinary act, she recovered her little homeland of repeated actions, of looking at her dolls, coffee and bread, radio, dishes to rinse.

The following Saturday, at her neighbour's house, she met the granddaughter, the television on low, a foreign newspaper on the table. She had a cut across her cheek, the granddaughter, but she seemed happy.

'People have started to bring mirrors to the protests.'

The granddaughter showed them a picture of a group of demonstrators before the Berkut, showing them their hard faces reflected in mirrors of all sizes. The blank stares of steel, looking to not look at themselves, looking to continue being what they were supposed to be without thinking much about it.

No-one will remember her, Luba Kushnir. No-one will know she was the first to carry the mirror that wanted to reflect humanity and not just hardness in Independence Square. But now, every time she washes herself after rinsing the dishes, she looks in it for a moment longer than necessary, Baba Luba, and feels companionship.

WINDOWS

It was that time of the winter evening when the sky is already pitch black, and she had just put the girl, the little one, to bed. I couldn't hear from home whether she had put on calming music, as she did sometimes in the summer, or whether she was letting the sounds of the city adorn the silence. It was the time of the evening when I would arrive home from work, pour myself a glass of wine, sit down in the dark, and watch her window from mine.

It was not a sick obsession. Just that one night, I caught sight of the woman working in the kitchen with a diligent expression, coming and going, seemingly singing or talking to herself in a low voice and a tranquil, docile pleasure rose in my belly. Within a few days, her routine was moulded to mine and I began to go out to dinner with friends only on Thursdays or Saturdays, when she was almost never home. During the months I observed her, I came to know whether she was happy or worried by the way she moved or the things she did.

That last evening she had a lively air about her, as if her whole body was singing. She could have been a ballerina: tall and slim, with small breasts and long legs. She was wearing kitchen gloves and was washing the dishes, completely unaware, unaware of her beauty in the yellow light, unaware of the world and of me and even herself.

Halfway through washing the dishes the phone must have rung. I couldn't hear it, but her phone rang, because she left the tap and the scrubber, glanced towards the marble counter on the left, and smiled. Then, as if unconcerned that it might stop ringing, she slowly removed a glove, just one, and her right hand — that I imagined to be soft and white, though I couldn't see it very well from the other side of the street — was naked.

Perhaps it was seeing her from afar, with none of the violence of annoying details, blurred by the night and the highest, thinnest branches of the pruned plane trees, that made her such a perfect image.

With her naked hand she grabbed the phone, pressed a button, and brought it close to her cheek. For a moment, only a moment, I'd have liked to be the voice that made her glow, that made her lean against a wall and breathe deeply, disarmed. For a moment I'd have liked to hear her voice, not just imagine it, telling me how her day had gone or what she'd do the next day.

I rose from the sofa, turned on the lamp, lowered the blind, and thought about eating something light and watching a long film. In the kitchen, the harshness of the fluorescent bulb made my hands blue.

RED

The loudest cries were fading so the panting of the others at the woman's side, and the orders from an older lady who seemed to be in charge could now be heard. The girl hadn't been attracted by the wailing; rather, she was looking for something to gnaw on and had stopped dead near the window on hearing how the woman was screaming. She hadn't come because of the screams, and it wasn't the screams that kept her rooted there. It was the blood.

She'd seen lots of blood, but not like that. These were big, dense clots of lighter blood. Crimson blood, living blood, blood. She was used to the dried, brownish blood of the dead people she'd stumble over just a few steps from home. Even when it was red it didn't shine that way, the dead blood of the men in uniform.

Those inside hadn't seen her, as they were preoccupied with attending the woman giving birth. So, she stayed there, unable to take her eyes off the tableau: the paling face of the woman, the blood on the sheets, on the midwives' aprons. How the streams running down her open legs were like sticky snakes. How what was sticking to the exasperated hands of the eldest woman was like damp earth.

The girl was there and they didn't see her, but not only because they were busy. She was looking so intensely at the scene that she had forgotten herself, and if breathing hadn't been a reflex action, if hearts didn't beat of their own accord however upset we are, she'd have died right there, without noticing. She'd become invisible.

The girl knew she shouldn't have seen all that. Even amid the horror of the siege there were things that grown-ups prefer children not to see. The girl was six or seven, and she was just looking for something to gnaw on. A crust of bread, a rind of cheese. A slice of something forgotten in a corner.

She often did that, roamed through houses looking for forgotten food. Sometimes she was lucky, but that day she found only blood, the woman giving birth ever whiter, the aprons ever redder. Now she'd fallen silent it was very quiet, and the stillness had infected the others. All of them, the girl too, were pillars of salt.

In silence, those inside looked at one another. The oldest put her cheek near the mouth of the woman. After a while had passed, she rolled up her sleeve and put her arm almost up to the elbow inside her. The girl knew she shouldn't have seen all that; the naked woman giving birth, unmoving except for some bulges in her belly that were rising and falling, as if there were a worm within, the midwife rummaging around in her insides. Finally, she withdrew her hand.

'Nothing to be done,' she said. Another old woman cried.

Then a foot stamping on the ground, a 'Let me', and the youngest woman pulling a knife from underneath her apron. A sharp knife that seemed to the girl to shine like the red snakes eating the legs of the woman giving birth, like the snakes that maybe she still had in her belly and that continued to bite the soft flesh no longer tensed in contractions.

The young woman brought the knife to the dead woman's belly, made an enormous cut, separated some entrails and, as if by magic, pulled out a wrinkled rabbit with no fur or floppy ears, a rabbit that was a baby.

He didn't cry straightaway. The young woman gripped him by the neck and wrapped him in a cloth. If within the belly he gave kicks that seemed strong enough to split it open, once outside he moved his arms slowly, as if it were difficult for him to drag them through the air. The old woman who was crying finally reacted. She grabbed the little one, kissed him, wet his face with her tears and prayers and pleas: 'Mother of God, don't take him from me, Mother of God, have mercy.'

No-one was looking at the disembowelled woman anymore.

Only the girl, still, white, and clutching her belly with her hands, as if any minute the young woman might come out and open her up too, pull out who knew what from her hunger swollen belly. When the little one coughed and began to cry, the women burst out in sobs which seemed to be of joy, while the postnatal woman remained silent. The girl took off running.

She ran far away, as far away as she could. Exhausted, she fell to the ground and hurt her knee, she covered her ears with her hands so as not to hear the cries that were no longer the laughter of the women, but were coming from her, they were her own disorientated sobs. A very thin snake of blood ran down to her ankle, red, shining.

She left the car, carelessly parked, beside the house. She liked parking like this when she went to the stone house where her grandmother had been born. She would park without concentrating, in the middle of the plot, because no one came to the house anymore. Only her, from time to time, when the city was suffocating and she needed to escape. The road to get there was full of stones and you had to go so slowly it would have maddened any visitor.

Taking out her suitcase, she thought of Arnaldo putting it on the back seat beside the basket of food, and her leaving the briefcase of painting tools on the front passenger seat of the yellow Dyane.

'You understand, right?' Gabriela had said.

He hadn't said anything. He'd hugged her, opened the car door for her, taken a step back. He'd stayed there and watched her start the car and move away.

Gabriela painted. In watercolour, in pastels, in oils, she painted on whatever paper she could find. She did it in order to not think at all, or for the very purpose of thinking. When she didn't have paper or a brush, she would paint in her head. That was why she had come to the house where her grandmother had been born; to paint. To be alone, to breathe. To forget about Arnaldo's secret meetings with other officials for a while, meetings from which one night he might not come back. To shake off the breathlessness in her chest, that the doctor said was asthma, an iron claw that kept her from sleeping.

She left the suitcase, the basket and the small case on the wooden table and opened the shutters on the windows. The house was simple: a kitchen with a fireplace and a living room on the ground floor, and two bedrooms above. Though her parents had done some renovations to make it more habitable, there was no bathroom, just a toilet in the backyard.

Arnaldo didn't like going there. It bothered him to the same degree that it enchanted Gabriela: it was a timeless place, far from the nearest village. No further comforts than silence, light and solitude. In the twenty years they'd been together she'd come maybe a couple of times with Arnaldo, and both times at the beginning.

This was fine with Gabriela. He always had things to do in Lisbon, and she could escape and go there whenever she wanted. She liked having a few hours of driving to the little house in Serra da Estela ahead of her and, whilst there, liked spending days and days without speaking to anyone. Painting, sleeping, going up to the brook, going down to the village to buy bread and cheese. Making a good fire if it was cold, reading by the love of the flames. Forgetting that she wasn't completely free.

She cleaned a little before settling in. Spring had officially arrived and there was no longer snow on the mountain, but there was still a nip in the air, and she liked to feel it coming through the open windows along with the sun. As she scrubbed the floor, she sang the songs her grandmother had taught her — *Sleep, sleep, little boy, your mother has things to do. She has lots of work, and not much to eat.* Almost all the songs her grandmother had taught her were lullabies or saucy poems which she would recite in secret, away from her father, because her grandmother knew that her son didn't like her to say such things in front of his little girl. They would laugh after every dirty word, and from the other side of the house her father must have known what they were doing, but he said nothing.

Gabriela had become an orphan with the death of her grandmother, as if nothing else but the house tied her to her family. She had inherited the stone house, and her northern cousins had become angry. Not because of the money, as it wasn't worth much, but because Gabriela, the eldest granddaughter, was the favourite, and even in death the old woman had to remind them of it. Gabriela had repeated that they could go there whenever they wanted, that Chica in the village bar had a copy of the keys. She kept telling them this until she became tired of repeating it and getting dirty looks, and eventually she didn't phone her northern cousins again.

Then she emptied the house of all the unwanted traces left behind from her cousins', her uncles' and aunts', even her parents' sporadic visits. She'd thrown away everything that didn't come from her grandmother's era so that entering the house was now like going back in time and finding a woman who cleans and sings, who places provisions in the food safe, who boils water in a pan, who sits down with a cup of tea on the stone bench attached to the wall beside the door and ponders the colour of the clouds that day.

Soon it was time to light the fire. She hadn't been late leaving Lisbon that morning, but it took a good few hours to get to the house and night had fallen without her realising. She toasted two slices of bread, nibbled a few olives, and poured herself a glass of wine. She picked up her book and lit the oil lamp, but she couldn't focus on reading. The best thing was to go to sleep, but once in bed she felt a stubborn restlessness in her belly that had no recognisable cause or quelled any thoughts.

The sun came up and found her still awake, tossing and turning in bed, wrapped in the house's yellowing sheets, the centuries-old coverlet. She decided to get up. Not even making a coffee, she put a sketchbook, a case with a few basic painting tools, and a couple of pieces of fruit in her backpack. And off she went uphill.

She felt she was looking for something, but didn't know what. She walked as if a force was pushing her. She knew the paths, the roads, the trails, but took each bend instinctively as if not choosing the route. Up, up, she walked for an hour, two. She arrived at the upper valley and her heart leapt when she heard the sheep bleating. She continued a little further and saw them, still faraway; she sat on a rounded rock and took out her sketchbook and a charcoal.

The flock seemed enormous to her, sheep and more sheep, with two sheepdogs leading the livestock. She'd seen sheep many times, of course. Her grandmother had always had them surrounding the house, just as there'd always been cheese in the pantry while she was alive. She'd known them since she was a little girl and had lived alongside them with the indifference provoked in us by habitual landscape. It was natural, finding sheep in the meadow, and she'd never felt an urge to draw them. That day, however, she looked at them with curiosity for the first time, like she was only just noticing them. The charcoal moved by itself. The grey, black, and white shadows of the meadow were just beginning to emerge from the winter, the grazing sheep began to appear on the paper.

She filled a sheet, two, ten, with the small eyes of the sheep, the woollen overcoat that would soon need to be shorn. The immense group occupying the meadow. Hooves, many hooves, stepping on the grass. The jaws moving up and down, chewing. One stretched out in the sun. Another pretending not to hear until it was herded by the dog and, resigned, returned to the others. Then she started a fresh page and, led by the charcoal, a silhouette emerged among the shadows. A man. Strong. Dark. With a few days' beard growth, with broad arms, with thick legs. Then Gabriela heard the whistle, raised her eyes from the paper and saw him.

He was still far away, and she couldn't make out his features; she was drawing him with the same intuition that had pushed her up the path, up there in the valley. She looked over the thick arms, black eyebrows, the nicked skin on his hands. She could have drawn him as she wanted him to be, but she drew him as she knew he was.

She wasn't sure whether he could see her from where he was, red backpack and all. She must be a dot in the landscape, alone, sitting on a rock, charcoal in hand. She looked at her last sketch, tidied away the sketchbook and took the road down towards home lightly, not noticing the hunger or the sleepless night in her body, not considering that if she went down too quickly her legs would hurt the following day.

The sun was high and she went outside to set up the broken easel her father had made for her when she began to paint as a little girl. She took her watercolours. She didn't need to look at the pad she had filled with shadows to paint all the tones of the yellowish wool; all the dark, minuscule, shining eyes; all the shades of green erupting in the valley.

She painted until there was no more light and, looking at the spread of sheets, she realised that they were all of beasts. She hadn't painted the man, even though in some way he was there. In the energy, the strength, the urgency with which she had painted: he was there.

She was ferociously hungry and ate the bread that was left over from the day before, the cured sausage she had brought from Lisbon, the fruit she hadn't finished that morning. She devoured everything she had and fell into bed, exhausted.

If she dreamed of anything that night, she didn't remember it the following day. She was awoken by the heat peaking at midday and decided to take advantage of the sun to bathe in the river. Sweaty, she headed towards the stream. Towel on one shoulder, she thought that he must do the same. He must smell of sheep, he too must bathe in the river.

The water was very cold. She stuck her foot into the small rockpool where she had bathed all her life with her grandmother, where the river descended peacefully, without violence; a current as transparent as the eyes of someone with nothing to hide. She put her feet in and the water reached her calves, a little below her knees. The cold stung her flesh, entering her bones and making her feel violently awake. She plunged her hands in, made a dish out of her cupped palms and threw the water on her face. Droplets trickled down her body giving her goosebumps, hardening her nipples, scratching her back. Droplets trickled down her body and she wanted more. She repeated the act many times, until she eventually stretched out on the pebbles of the river floor and was so frozen she stopped breathing.

Submerged in the merciless cold, time seemed to lengthen. She imagined the shepherd looking at her and opened her legs. She felt icy needles on her skin, as if every inch of her was raw flesh. 'That's it,' she said to herself, 'all of me raw flesh, all of me alive, flesh.'

She rose slowly and with ceremony, like Venus being born in the river, and left the water. Beneath the improvised layer of an old towel, she was shivering. She hugged her knees and kissed them, and once over the first cold, lay out in the sun and let the warmth lick the wounds made by the freezing water.

She had her eyes closed, her eyelids were two orange spots, curtains that shut out the sky, a protective capsule, a wall that made everything invisible but the beating of her heart. 'Your heartbeat is very strong,' Arnaldo had told her the first evening they had made love. She hadn't known whether he was saying it admiringly or with a little fear, but now she thought it was both. If he could see her now, wild by the river, he would both admire and fear her.

She heard the sound of sheep passing on the track and let them go by. She heard the dogs barking, she heard footsteps coming closer, she felt a shadow cover her face. She didn't open her eyes. She just stayed still, like the river, living flesh with a heartbeat that was too strong. The shadow left.

The cow bells were fading away. After a while she went back to only hearing the insects, the running water, the breeze moving some bushes. Dressing, her clothes felt strange against her skin. Without haste, breathing deeply to fill her lungs with every gulp of air, she headed home. At the entrance she found a small bunch of toadflax, green splashed with purple, on the stone bench. She put it on her lapel.

Perhaps it was the hunger and the empty larder, or perhaps it was a desire to see herself reflected in the eyes of others. I'm part of the tribe, me too. I draw beasts, I swim naked, but I'm part of the tribe. She tidied herself up a little, took the car and went down to the village for dinner. As always, the same group of people were in the bar, and when old Chica heard Roldao greeting her, she came out of the kitchen to receive her with great ceremony, big hugs, and shouts of alarm because she was thinner and must eat.

She had dinner in the kitchen while Chica told her the village gossip and answered Roldao from time to time that: yes, the soup was coming. As it got late, they closed and Gabriela stayed there in Chica's kitchen, helping her wash the dishes. Their conversation had dwindled but they kept each other company, as if it were hard for both of them to say goodbye.

When they finished clearing up, Chica switched on the radio and brought out a bottle of liqueur and three small glasses. Roldao sat with them, happy to see the granddaughter of Albertina from the house in the valley, happy to still be alive. He began to tell stories of when they were young, insinuating that he could have courted Albertina. Chica elbowed him mockingly and told him not to tell so many lies and that on the first day of school he had glanced at her and fallen in love.

It must have been after twelve. And that song she'd liked so much at the Amalia Rodrigues concert she'd gone to with Arnaldo two or three weeks ago came on — *em cada esquina um amigo, em cada rosto igualdade*. Arnaldo, too, had fallen in love with her on the first day of school, or almost, though she'd noticed him much later.

A sombra duma azinheira que ja nao sabia a idade , sang the radio, and Gabriela remembered how she'd come home alone in a taxi the night of the concert because Arnaldo was going 'for a couple of drinks' with the other officials. She knew that the drinks were an excuse to speak of everything they couldn't discuss in the barracks, and that night she stayed up waiting for him.

He arrived home restless, very late. Gabriela undressed him, kissed his eyelids, laid him on the bed. And he let her do it, do-cile as he usually was when she sought him, but not afterwards. Afterwards he took the reins, bound her wrists with his strong hands, took her with a hard and cruel need.

They hadn't spoken that night; they almost never spoke. But still, she felt very close to him and it must have been the song and the memory of being embraced, smoking and watching the dawn filling the bed with light that made her drink up her liqueur and rise.

She didn't return to the house to close the shutters, or to get her suitcase and gather the few things she had left scattered around. She went south, towards Lisbon, and drove calmly, with a finger of her window down to let the fresh night air in. Living flesh coming home, a beating heart that knows the way.

She arrived in Lisbon early in the morning but couldn't get close to home. The streets had been taken by people who were singing, raising their fists and shouting enough war, enough soldiers. She had to leave the car in a street she didn't know, let herself be carried by the crowd of people that were smiling drunkenly; why, she wasn't quite sure. With the feeling of history changing, the feeling of having the army on their side, the feeling that a very long night was about to end.

'Gabriela!'

She turned. There was Arnaldo, hanging off a truck, smiling. He seemed younger, rumpled, the shirt of his uniform unbuttoned.

'You haven't brought me carnations from the market, like everyone else?'

She looked at the flowers, removed them from her lapel, and offered him the toadflax. She accepted the hands he offered her and climbed onto the truck. Laughing at her man's side, she went all over the living city that was beating hard, flesh exhilarated by spring.

SYBILLE

They were beautiful, the boots she had in her hands. I entered the workshop and she didn't kick me out. I entered the workshop and sat down before her, watching her as she silently worked the leather in her hands. I didn't say anything, and neither did she.

Weeks ago, I passed by the small shop-studio every day on my way to the local bar. For the first few days after losing my job, I'd go there almost hopefully. I'd talk to friends and after the third beer it seemed to us that we had great schemes, that we'd create a thousand different companies and provide work for the whole neighbourhood. They were stillborn, those companies, and we reduced the cold corpse of the half-baked idea with: 'Another beer then, Lluïsa.' We were on the verge of it all and everything seemed possible, except that we remained indefinitely on the verge of it all, in the realm of possibility, where words promised much, but our hands did little.

It didn't take long for the gatherings to become less cheerful. My friends and I fell quiet until a new person arrived, and for a while it would seem some still wanted to believe it. But not me. I kept going to the bar and hardly drank anymore. I'd sit in a corner and watch the old men playing dominoes, bite my nails, go over to the noticeboard, re-read the same offers of work a thousand times. I no longer despaired. I just kept quiet and slowly nibbled the peanuts Lluïsa would slip me when the boss wasn't looking.

Very early one day, painfully sober, and roaming around the neighbourhood so as not to be at home, I stopped in front of the workshop's large window and I thought the boots she was making were beautiful. I thought it would be nice to watch her working all day and, having all day, I went in.

She didn't kick me out or say anything, she barely even looked at me. She kept working with her small, strong hands and her hardened fingertips ran over the pieces of leather so naturally that it seemed easy. At mid-morning she rose from the table, went to a corner, boiled water and came back with two herbal teas. She offered me one.

When I had been there hours, without moving, just watching her, she said: 'Stay here a minute.'

She didn't need anyone to stay anywhere, but I was filled with a warm glow by this gesture of giving me a place, in her way, without much needing to be said. From time to time she would send me to run errands, slowly but surely teaching me the job. She even started to pay me a little.

And so she made me the shoemaker's assistant. She did so without offering me the position, not even asking herself if she wanted the help, just assuming that anyone who spent so many hours watching her work must want to learn the trade.

And how beautiful it was, watching her work... She didn't repair shoes or glue soles that immediately came unstuck from cheap factory-made shoes. No, Sybille made shoes to measure, by hand, one by one. She made shoes that fitted the feet wearing them, like a glove. She made shoes that were caresses, putting all her care into them.

I'd studied for many years, done office work all my life. I wasn't expecting to be anyone's apprentice, and even less the shoemaker's assistant. In the silence of the long hours in the workshop, with no radio, with nothing more than the sewing machine and tools to remind us that we hadn't lost our hearing, I learned the pleasure of handling the leather, smelling it, sewing it.

I still wear them, the boots Sybille was finishing that day. Old and worn as they are, I still wear them, and they are a second skin kissing away my fatigue at the end of the day. She told me as she stretched them out that they were too tight for the client who had ordered them. But when I put my feet in them, I knew she had also observed me as I passed by every day, and from afar she'd been able to work out my measurements.

Here, lad, these are yours. I'll not pretend otherwise, I started them as soon as I saw you stop before the workshop window for the third time. And when you came in and sat down before me, I knew for certain what Sybille also knew with me. I think we know, we true shoemakers, who will learn the trade from us.

Take them, these are your boots. Wear them well.

Being the Lady of the Snow isn't easy. I don't like the name, for a start. Snow is cold and I don't like the cold, and when I was up there, so frozen I was no longer shivering, one of the last things I remember thinking was that freezing to death was a double punishment for someone who hated the cold. I thought I was dying even though it seems not. Or I was. But now, in this world, with these people, it's possible to bring a well-preserved body back to life. And so mine was, when they found it.

I should never have gone to the snow, and now I am the Lady of the Snow. I wanted to go to the beach, toast myself in the sun, read trashy magazines and knock a ball back and forth with my feet in the water. Sleep a lot, think very little, not move too much. The fact is I ended up in the snow and the cord broke, and Josep and the others were further, further, ever further away while I was falling and eventually I could no longer hear their voices. After the fall, once the unbearable pain in my back subsided, I thought a helicopter would come, that I'd surely be saved. But no. Centuries passed and these cheerful, slightly odd females ended up coming, and I am now the Lady of the Snow, forever and ever, because it seems that here you don't die if you don't want to.

The house they've given me is comfortable. I can transform it however I like. I'm not really sure how it works but, if I want, I can convert it into a tropical garden, or a jungle, and get lost in it. I can even put mosquitoes in there if I like, because they say people like me, who come from times in which time was important, miss the inconveniences when they're not there. But the truth is I like that they're not there. They say it will come in time, that one day I'll grow bored of the perfection that makes them happy and yearn for everything I used to hate, because people like me, they say, have it deeply ingrained in them that everything perfect must be unreal, and no one likes to feel that what they are experiencing is unreal. It appears that everyone they've rescued from various places (all frozen in circumstances resembling my own) have ended up asking to die. I think I want to be the exception that proves the rule.

At the moment, I accept it all as a dream. I always liked dreaming in my other life, centuries and centuries ago. Many times, I knew perfectly well that I was dreaming, and I was able to go and see friends who were faraway, or fly, or eat exactly what I felt like eating. Here is somewhat similar: you open the console and tell it what you want. Sometimes it's difficult because the translator isn't perfect, or because what you're asking for isn't catalogued, but generally it works well. In the early days I played with changing the colour of the furniture or walls, but for a while now I've found myself comfortable with these warm tones and it feels less strange to me if I don't change them. My house has walls, but their houses don't. Their houses are like desert islands or unending meadows or moons on a night full of stars. Their houses have no visible limits, but they like the space, and with the console they can tear down walls and make horizons to measure. Mine has them because they say the others, those like me, preferred them. I've kept them because the idea of infinity is irreparably linked to inclement weather and in this life I tolerate the cold even less than in the other.

I haven't really connected with them yet. Only Sunno, who has a kind of obsession with my time and knows things I didn't even know about my world, visits me every day and invites me every so often to what might be described as a party. Sunno has been in charge of almost all those found, and perhaps the experience of so many deaths (absurd in her opinion) has changed her slightly, humanised her a little. I say this and realise I'm judging them, making them out to be less human than we are, when it could actually be the complete opposite. But the genesis of this perfectly balanced world, in which everyone has what they want without treading on anyone's toes, in which resources are infinite because they never stop existing completely, like all geneses, is more than a little dark.

It's not totally clear how it happened, because a long time ago the founding mothers decided to die. But what is known now is that one day, the way of living forever was discovered. In the beginning there were all the problems Vonnegut imagined in his *2BR02B*: over-population, scarcity of resources, chaos. And they started solving them as he proposed: extreme birth control and a dictatorship. But then a group of women decided enough was enough. Sunno hasn't been able to explain to me why only women, why not a single man stood out in that drastic revolt. The fact is that some two hundred people, silently, methodically and suddenly, exterminated the rest of humanity. They were convinced that a fairer, calmer, healthier world was possible. And they achieved it.

No one knows how they did it, although the most plausible hypothesis is that they used a sonic weapon resembling that used by Pedrolo's aliens in *Typescript of the Second Origin*.

In their underground refuge, far from the orgy of death they'd created, they established the basis of the new society. The death penalty applies to anyone breaking the law, because the law is just, necessary, consensual, universal. Total freedom to each person in their realm — their house — as long as they don't hurt anyone.

I suppose that's why they live in such isolation. It's difficult to have a relationship without getting hurt. I suppose that's why for a long time, despite the possibilities offered by the self-fertilisation techniques used by their ancestors, none of the hundred thousand inhabitants of this world has thought of having children. I suppose that's why they have robots programmed to each person's taste as romantic companions, which can be re-programmed to be more in love every day. I suppose that's why Sunno sometimes looks at me fearfully when I talk to her about what embracing is like, what body warmth is really like. I suppose that's why I hate being the Lady of the Snow and would much prefer — a thousand times more — to be the Lady of Fire.

LINDA

SANTA ROSA — She fires the last bullet and knows she has to run. She hasn't hit them all and now they're not moving because they're still afraid, but if she stands there they'll realise she has no more bullets and come after her. Apart from some pitiful moans, she's surprised by the silence she's made until she's woken by the horn of someone about to knock her down and so realises it wasn't silence, but just a state of shock, and the moans weren't coming from any of the boys, but from her.

She looks at her clothes and searches for blood but can't find any, only the warm pistol in her hand, her finger painful after pulling the trigger so hard. She runs, runs towards home, and halfway there she thinks, no, not home, better somewhere else. She knocks on Jenny's door and, while waiting for her to open it, she looks at her clothes again, because it seems incredible that there's no blood, and pulls down her skirt which has ridden up as she ran.

Jenny opens the door and smiles, *hello hello*, but then her face changes and she screams something and pulls her inside. Her friend tries to wrench the gun from her hand but though she wants to she can't let it go and her finger keeps gripping and hurting more and more.

Jenny drags her down the hall and gets her into the shower. When the cold water falls onto her she thinks tears will also fall, that she'll let go of the pistol and it will fall to the ground, but it's not that simple. She looks at the water flowing down in a whirlpool and it surprises her that it is transparent; she keeps thinking that blood must be oozing from somewhere in her body.

Jenny tells her she can't lift her out of the shower alone, that she'll have to help, so she raises one foot and then the other, takes off the wet clothes, and allows herself to be wrapped in a towel. The pistol is still there, and Jenny takes her hand and forcibly opens her fingers one by one, and they give way until her palm is open. Her hand is rigid and the pistol has vanished because Jenny has taken it from her side.

She stands there, looking at her hand, as if she might see her destiny in the lines. The lifeline, the loveline. She can't remember what that other shorter one is, but she knows it's important. And she doesn't need to know palmistry to divine her future: they'll find her, they'll put her in prison, and she'll rot there. Maybe when the police detain her they'll decide to have a little fun, but she doesn't have bullets any more, she doesn't even have the pistol, only her right hand, painful and absurdly white when there should have been blood.

Jenny comes back with dry clothes and she puts them on while Jenny says nothing, doesn't ask what happened, doesn't try to make her talk. She imagines she must look a state because Jenny is silent, and she always talks and talks and talks. But sooner or later she'll have to explain to someone what has happened, and better it be Jenny.

The telephone rings and both of them jump. Jenny goes over to it, not even clearing her throat, as if she's certain a nice normal 'Hello' will come out, and it does. She's in the living room but from the bathroom she hears a nice normal 'Hello.' 'No, no, she's not here. No way. Really? Ok. I'll let you know. Ok. Bye.'

And she says it was Pablo, that he's looking for her. The whole neighbourhood is looking for her, maybe the whole city. The police, for sure, and her father, who says this time he will kill her, and Pablo, who wants to help her.

'Girl, you're crazy,' says Jenny. 'You killed two guys and injured three more, another one broke his leg while trying to escape.' She thinks that's okay, good enough aim — in the country with Pablo, she never used to hit the cans.

She realises that she should be feeling something she isn't, some kind of empathy for the lives she has cut short. But she only feels a touch of pride (got five of them) and fear (killed two) — they'll give her a long sentence. She also feels a lot of rage and thinks that the easy way out would be to kill herself with her new-found aim, but she doesn't have bullets or even the pistol anymore.

The phone rings again and Jenny goes over and answers it. 'Yeah, Pablo told me. No, I don't know anything. Yes, I'll keep you posted.' And after the third call she turns off her mobile and brings it into her room, not knowing when her parents might get home. She sits on the bed and Jenny brings her a herbal tea, but it's too hot and the warm tea makes her sweat a heat that penetrates her like that of the pistol in her hand.

Jenny doesn't want to give her back the pistol. 'It needs to be well-cleaned and thrown away somewhere. You're crazy, as if you haven't done enough harm already. Girl, why did you kill them? They're saying that they'd greeted you, that maybe they'd said something to you, nothing out of the ordinary. And you came back soon afterwards and started firing.'

She'd like to explain why to her, but it wouldn't sound logical now. The phone is switched off because otherwise it wouldn't stop ringing, and she is sitting on Jenny's bed in her clothes, with this heat within that's making her sweat. She'd like to explain why to her but then she'd start to cry, or the rage would come back. And she doesn't have a pistol anymore.

SABADELL — 'There are words one shouldn't utter because they can lead to fatal consequences. This thought didn't cross the minds of two twenty-year-old Venezuelans who couldn't resist the charms of a woman. So far, the story could be the beginning of a soap opera.'

The paper is free and Lola reads it because today the sudoku was easy and she finished it immediately; she still has twenty minutes of her journey left to kill. The headline caught her eye: 'A young woman kills two men for some poisoned catcalls'. It seems unbelievable that so many stereotypes could fit into so few words, three short paragraphs. 'We still don't know why the young woman reacted this way,' say the police officers in charge of the investigation. Yes, that's the problem right there, thinks Lola; they really don't understand.

Lola only wanted to pass the time, do the sudoku, read some titbits of news that would keep her entertained until work, and so she's skipped the politics and economic sections. But now she's somewhere between sad and cross, she thinks about the girl, what will happen to her, and the poor unfortunates that have died without understanding anything, how the police will continue living.

She needs to alight at the next station and so gets up, moves to the door and waits for the train to stop. She goes up the long escalators, thinking about what she needs to do at work today, mentally organising everything pending before the weekend. She emerges onto the street and it's warm for being only eight in the morning, and she thinks summer this year has gone on for long enough.

'Lower your skirt, love — you're turning me on! Ah, if I got you in a dark alley…'

Lola stops dead, turns. From the top of a ladder, the man winks at her, as if he doesn't know how to interpret the woman's face full of rage, as if he doesn't see it. Slowly, Lola goes over to the ladder. The man smiles. Lola grabs it, tries to sway it, but it weighs too much to do so in a controlled way. She could certainly push it and make him fall. Now he's shouting at her, insulting her. She looks up, smiles, leaves him the newspaper open on the Venezuelan article at the foot of the ladder. The man doesn't understand, won't understand anything.

Lola takes her headphones from her bag and puts on a song nice and loud and struts as if the street were hers.

NEW YORK — Something had to be done, I said to myself, and I did the only thing I know: paint. Something had to be done and

I painted portraits of my girlfriends first, then of many other women. As I painted them they would talk to me, tell me their experiences. Without seeking them, slogans were emerging:

STOP TELLING WOMEN TO SMILE. I'M NOT WALKING DOWN THE STREET FOR YOUR PLEASURE. CRITICISM OF MY BODY IS NOT APPRECIATED. MY NAME IS NOT GIRLIE, OR GORGEOUS, OR BLONDIE, OR GOOD-LOO- KING. I AM NOT STREET FURNITURE. I DON'T OWE YOU A SECOND.

I put a phrase under each portrait and printed them on enor- mous posters. Walking through Brooklyn, the first time that I came across one I wasn't expecting, it affected me deeply. It was Sarah, a head and shoulders portrait, three metres by seven, and in huge letters: I'M NOT YOURS.

I sat on the steps in front for a while and felt protected by that powerful giant, staring straight into the eyes of whoever looked at her, sending a clear message. I sat there for a while and without really knowing why, I started to cry.

'Are you okay?'

It was a girl of my own age, short like me, black like me, friendly like me. I nodded and she sat beside me for a moment, we looked at the poster together. We kept each other company for a few minutes, and then she left.

INVISIBLE

It's 5.40 a.m. when the alarm clock buzzes. I'd like to throw it out of the window, but there's no window and I have to get up anyway, so I stop it, get up and grab my clothes and bag and jacket from the chair so I don't have to go back in and annoy the two newbies, snoring a little in the bed above mine, apparently oblivious to the alarm clock that has just gone off. By 5.46 I'm in the kitchen and I wash the cafetiere to make coffee, a cup to put the coffee in, and a teaspoon to stir the sugar into the coffee. I open the fridge to grab the leftovers from yesterday's dinner, but someone must have eaten them. At 6.02 Luana arrives and goes straight to the bedroom. When I emerge from the icy shower at 6.16, there's already no sound from the bedroom which must mean she is sleeping.

At 6.25 I pass what used to be a living room and is now another bedroom with four beds, all with sleeping occupants. I go down to the street and it's cold so I rummage in all my jacket pockets to see if I can find a coin which might buy me a spell in a café, but no. So I take Carrer Hospital and come to the Rambla where I go up and up until I'm in Plaça Catalunya and go underground to the Renfe train station. I sit on the floor for a while, close my eyes for a moment, and remember today is Friday and Juanjo will pay me, I can buy something for dinner and pay rent for another week, maybe I'll go to a cybercafé and be online with my mother for a while, it's been days now since I last spoke to her.

It's almost 6.57 and I start on the eight o'clock shift, so I get up and when the attendants aren't watching I slip in behind an old-timer, I feel bad because I have to push him a little. I say 'Sorry' to him politely, he curses youth but doesn't hit me because he's not strong enough and doesn't spit at me because his dentures would fall out, but he does look at me in a way I'd never want anyone to look at me. I catch the 7.04 train, though the 7.13 would get me there in plenty of time, and the heating and people warm me up so much that I take off my jacket — I get a whiff of the soap I used that morning from my t-shirt, and I'm happy for having showered, even if it was with icy water. At 7.28 the train arrives at the suburb where the factory is and I get off and slip through again to exit, this time behind a boy who makes out that he hasn't noticed.

After a ten-minute walk I arrive at the industrial estate and enter the third warehouse. It's early, 7.42, but I go to the changing room, take off my jacket, put on the overcoat, and then I sit on the bench until 7.57, because Juanjo doesn't like us to arrive early or late. I go over to the machine and say hello to Jasmina, she gets out, and I get in. Time passes until 13.59 when it's time to stop for lunch, and Maica comes to relieve me. And then, while I am looking at my nails on the bench outside, because someone ate the leftovers from my dinner and I have nothing at all to eat, Juanjo comes and tells me I can clock off, there's not much work, that my weekly pay is in the envelope, and that if there's anything, he'll call. But I don't have a phone and I know he's just saying that to say something. I go to the changing room, get my jacket, put it on over my overcoat and retrace my steps to the train. In the station bar I buy myself a pork sandwich with cheese and, feeling flush, I even buy a ticket. It's 14.46 and it's a beautiful afternoon, the winter sun so soft that it could be someone's hands stroking my hair through the train window. And suddenly, seeing the faraway dirty chimney stacks of Barcelona, I don't know why, but I slam my hand hard against the glass, and the face of my watch cracks, and I start laughing so hard that everyone in the carriage looks at me, and for a moment it's as if I truly existed in that city where every day so many people live without living.

THREE

There was a time when, if she'd done the night shift, the little ones would jump on her when she opened the front door. Still in pyjamas, they'd leave the television and run to her as soon as they heard the key in the lock and the creak of the door, which was never well-oiled.

Then the girls grew up and a calm, no-nonsense indifference emerged, which she supposed was normal. Adolescence, yada yada, yada. They grew up and didn't stop loving her, but they didn't show it so much anymore. They didn't like to see her come home worn out from work and would continue eating breakfast facing the television even once she'd arrived. They would mumble a half-hearted good morning through cereal and yoghurt, and then one, normally Cèlia, would get up to go for a shower and give her an indifferent kiss.

There were three of them: triplets. Cèlia was the smallest, as if her docile nature had made her shrink to leave space for the others in her mother's belly and she'd never managed to grow fully. Sandra and Berta would just as soon over-protect her as align themselves against her, but their mother didn't usually intervene. They will sort it out themselves, Carme would think, and look away so as not to see the little one's imploring eyes.

She used to do the night shift seven days in a row, then have three off. Then it would be her turn for the morning shift, seven days in a row, three days off. The one she liked least was the evening shift; she got home when the girls were in bed, Marc would be tired, and the following day she'd spend all morning putting on washing, cleaning, making lunches and dinners for when she wasn't at home.

The girls didn't know what her work was, then. Marc felt they were too young, it embarrassed Carme to talk about it, and they didn't ask. They waited as long as they could, and perhaps it was postponing that moment that contributed to the girls' distance, the reason that when they thought she didn't see them they looked at her differently, as if she were an impostor, as if she had deceived them, as if working and being the breadwinner were a terrible sin.

At work, the most difficult thing — at the time when the girls would jump on her when she opened the front door — was to not kiss, hug and cradle the children in the unit. Most of them were a little younger than her daughters. Like all children, they had runny noses and their shoelaces came undone, but she couldn't run after them with a tissue, or sit them on her lap and re-tell the story that rose to the tip of her tongue every time she tied a shoelace: *here is one ear, here is the other, here are the mouse's whiskers.* The children — her children — loved it. 'Mummy, mummy, tell us the story about the mouse when you're tying our shoes.' Velcro shoes arrived much later, and she was happy that fashion hadn't snatched away their childhood.

With the children — her children — she'd do *Five Little Ducks* and sing *Ten in the Bed* and they knew they had to take turns but Berta always tried to sneak in first and Cèlia would often let her. Though she'd be tired when she came home in the morning, she'd play with them for a while until Marc told them it was time to get dressed — *you'll be late for school* — and she'd have liked it to always be Sunday and be able to stay put in the middle of the dining room, with the girls in pyjamas, making up the lyrics she couldn't remember.

Sundays in the unit were sadder than other days. Not much was different, and this was what made them sadder. Visits were on Saturdays, and on Sunday those who'd had one missed their families all the more, and those who hadn't were happy to watch the lucky ones pretend they weren't broken; rage is the ultimate refuge when you don't have anything else on hand to hold onto.

If she was off, Sunday was the day she took the girls to the park. There was a quite a big one not very far from home with a pond they called the lake that had some ducks swimming on it. They would bring stale bread they had kept all week if they knew that Mummy was off on Sunday, and she would sit on a bench while the girls threw crusts from a plastic bag. Marc didn't usually go with them, taking the chance to relax, but the few times he'd accompanied them the girls' eyes shone brighter and they would fight to be between Daddy and Mummy at the same time, holding their hands.

In the unit on Sundays, they would put on a children's film. It was always old, the sound was always bad, and it always skipped. The children in the unit had never seen a duck, a real one, had never brought them bread. In the unit they didn't keep leftover food, everything was thrown away. There were very few things that could be kept in the cells. The inmates didn't have much either.

The children were with their mothers until they were three years old, and then they were taken away. To a relative's home, if they had any. To a children's home if they were unlucky. The majority couldn't be adopted; their mothers would take charge of them when they got out. And there weren't many welcoming families. She'd imagine the children going to the park on Sundays to give stale bread to the ducks. Some of them came back to visit their mothers on Saturdays with their grandmother, or more rarely, their father. Some suffered so much that after a few weeks they stopped bringing them for visits. She'd see them from afar, touch the hanky in her pocket, not offer it to them, breathe.

Maira's daughter, Paola, reminded her of her Cèlia. She knew that if the others were in the yard, when she found a toy that she liked, she had to play with it in secret. If not, it would always end up in other hands: someone bigger, stronger, more certain of their right to it. The others didn't have to hit her to get her to give them the toy. They would just say: 'It's mine', and she would hand it over, even though nothing there belonged to anyone, even though everything there, almost always, had been someone else's before. She would hand over the toy and look around with imploring eyes, and the jailer, if she saw her, would look away.

She'd practically been born there, Paola, shut in with her mother for drug-trafficking. Nothing too serious, a few grams, but a repeat offender and surly. The little girl was a year younger than the triplets and she sometimes wore the clothes that Carme brought to the prison when they'd outgrown them. Paola didn't know that her favourite dress had also been Cèlia's, and had never dirtied it in the mud of the pond.

When she saw her in the dress, proud, a joy rose in Carme that immediately faded, leaving a hollow within her. Afterwards, this hollow was difficult to fill. She would come home, play with her daughters, not let on. And then some child from the unit would turn three, or one would come back again, and the well would expand once more.

She didn't allow herself much of a relationship with the children in the unit. If she could have avoided it, she wouldn't have even learned their names. But there were so few of them, and she saw them every day. She could recognise Benji's nervous laugh, Mari's repetitive singing, Pepín's bitter tears. Officially, no-one warned them when the children were to leave until the last day, but normally they'd know beforehand because the mothers became even more irritable, or cried all day, or requested a visit from a legal aid lawyer, as if anything could be done.

They'd make them a cake with three candles, and they'd blow them all out. And afterwards, whatever wish they'd made, they would be taken away, not understanding anything. For many it would be the first time on the outside. Carme wondered if at night they found themselves missing the muffled sounds of nearby cells, or if rubbish trucks startled them in the middle of the night. Certainly, certainly they would miss their mother's body.

It was a Sunday the day the girls — her girls — turned three, and to be reminded less of the ritual at work she bought them sparklers. 'We can't blow them out, Mum,' they complained. 'It's fine, there's no need to cry,' said Cèlia. And Carme went into the kitchen to look for the previous year's candles, to give them at least one that they could blow out together. She went into the kitchen to let the tears flow freely, to not feel Marc's accusatory glance, *you always bring work home with you.*

There was a time when, if she'd done the night shift, the little ones would jump on her when she opened the front door. Today she finds the house empty. It's the last day she'll come home from work, and they've given her a watch that she's carrying in the box where she put the few things she had in her locker. Perhaps in the evening she'll call the girls, ask if they want to go to the park with the grandkids on Sunday, she'll keep stale bread all week.

SAND THROUGH HER FINGERS

She lets the sand run through her fingers and makes it fall onto her feet in a cascade that begins slowly, growing ever faster, until there's almost nothing left in her hand, and it goes back to dropping slowly, unwilling to leave her palms. Just like when she was a little girl, she lets the sand fall through her fingers onto her feet, burying them. It's thicker, this sand, and doesn't form that white powder that covered everything, that mixed with salt and aged spades, buckets, rakes. She grabs another handful and half opens her fingers. Useless, an eternal hourglass that doesn't tell time.

She looks at her real watch, the one on her wrist, and still has three quarters of an hour before going back to work. She doesn't turn but feels the shadow of the building — in town they call it 'the centre' without needing to specify what exactly it is 'the centre' of. It's as if there were no other centre, nor could the place be anything else. The building is just a discreet mass of concrete that could be an A&E or a library. There are few windows and a closed-off, yet discreet yard. She saw it for the first time a little over a month ago. It seemed strangely inoffensive to her, on one side of the avenue, between palm trees, with sea views. Once inside, it was different.

Forty-five minutes: she could bathe for a moment and still have time to dry off. The beach, past the stream at one end of the town, is empty. October is ending, people are back at work, the mass of tourists have gone home, and the retirees stroll along the other side where there are more benches and more bars and more life. Most people here are those who come to leisurely walk their dog, but not mid-morning in this blazing sun. She could bathe for a moment; her black underwear would pass for a bikini if anyone saw her. She thinks about it absently until she realises she's thinking about it, and decides it's better not to waste time if she's going to do it. She brushes off the sand still on her hands, stands up and takes off her trousers and t-shirt.

Walking a few steps, she feels water that is warmer than she was expecting. She enters the sea little by little, letting the waves break against her knees, her stomach, and her shoulders. She dives. She swims to the buoy and back, as she has done every summer on so many beaches. But she stops at the buoy, does the dead man's float, and hears, with the water covering her ears, distorted sounds she doesn't recognise. She closes her eyes, disappearing.

It's not exactly happiness, more an oblivion from within herself that she misses when it fades away, sometimes painfully, sometimes resignedly. Today, it fades away quickly with a niggle in her stomach from an automatic internal alarm: it must be late, she needs to get back. She quickly swims to the shore without looking at her watch and reaches the scarf spread out as if it were a towel. She is exhausted. Now looking at the time, she awards the sun ten minutes. She'll still have a quarter of an hour to get to her class.

She makes the most of the time. Two minutes to shake herself down, get dressed, get her things together. Three to cross the road and walk towards the fence. One and a half to greet the guard on camera, push the door and go to the toilet at the entrance. Three to wash her hands and face, pull her hair back into a ponytail, look at herself in the mirror and turn away before ceding to the strangeness produced by seeing herself lately. Two to go to the classroom. And done, already there. One minute and a half before the time she's expected, leaning against the wall, beside the door. She feels the salt on her skin, the damp underwear under her trousers. She hears Dolors giving homework, unconvincing arguments from Pedro and Ahmed knowing they won't do it anyway. She hears the bell striking twelve o'clock. Dolors comes out, they greet one another, she enters, forcing a smile. *One hour till lunchtime, boys and girls, almost there.*

When she received the posting, Paul insisted it wasn't necessary for her to take it. 'I earn enough, it'll be chaos. It'll be very hard for the children. I'll need help. Between petrol, rent and childcare, it'll be as if you're not earning anything. You'll find something else, we'll get through it.' A very long list of reasons, all sensible, objectively valid, perfectly reasonable. But before the definitive posting, which she hoped would be closer to home, she had to undergo months of work experience. She had taken a long time to sit the exams (Teo was a baby, Paul was doing his thesis, then Lua was a baby, Paul had his viva) and had passed them by the skin of her teeth (taking Teo to drumming, editing Paul's articles, taking Lua to the swimming pool, Paul's trips). She was pushed a little by pride — *I don't plan on being a kept woman* — but above all by the suffocation that prevented her from continuing to let herself be meekly carried away by life as she had for so long. 'It's work, and with how things are I can't say no. If I don't do the work experience, I may as well not have done anything. Who knows when they will convene exams again? It will only be a few months. I'll be home from Friday to Monday.' And it wasn't discussed any further.

In winter the cost of renting an apartment in that beach town is ridiculous. It didn't take long to find the right one: two rooms, a living room with an open kitchen, tiny bathroom. A little terrace, WiFi and a communal garden, sea views. Far away, between the gaps left by the gigantic seafront buildings, sea views. Five minutes on foot to the beach, three minutes on foot from the supermarket, two hours and fifty minutes in the car from home.

'Miss, this book doesn't have letters.'

'Yes it has, but they're weird.'

'This is shit. I'm not doing it.'

They talk as if she weren't there, because she isn't fully there. Her mind is still at the buoy, or rather her mind is longing for the buoy, longing to float under the sky. But they talk as if she weren't there, and this brings her back to the class, to the seven copies of the book she has managed to get the centre to buy, even though they are expensive, even though there's no money: one copy between two, and if they promise to behave themselves, they can choose their partners.

She's chosen a graphic novel, with no text other than the title, because while the class is, in theory, year 10, Miqui and Salva can hardly read a complete sentence, Salma only arrived recently, and no-one knows if she understands anything because she doesn't speak, and for the majority of them it's very difficult to read and they are so negative about the whole thing that she thought a book like that, *The Arrival*, would be easier to work with.

'Let's see, Rosina says there are letters. Where are they?'

'Here, Miss, see them? He's put something here.'

'And what do you think it says, Rosina?'

'I don't know. Passport, maybe? It looks like a passport.'

'Fuck, so why don't they put "passport" then for fuck's sake.'

'Could be that the guy is an illustrator but doesn't know how to write, so his letters are weird.'

'Or it could be that we don't know this language, because it's from another country. Chinese or something.'

They hypothesise in Spanish: Chinese isn't like that; one invented a secret alphabet with her brother as a little girl; one thinks it doesn't matter, the book can be understood even if it doesn't say anything — *it's like a film, before there used to be silent films, I swear man, whatever, films where they didn't speak, what a load of shit.*

She lets them follow the protagonist's journey — a man who migrates — and doesn't get too involved, only imposing order when it seems they're beginning to fight with each other, asking them questions that can help them interpret the book. They had complained at the beginning of the class, because it seems obligatory to complain about everything at that age, but the book piques their curiosity and engages them: it isn't like any book they've leafed through before. She feigns the same indifference as they do, she doesn't show even the slightest sign of the satisfaction of seeing them enjoy themselves, and soon

65

it's time to finish. Deborah collects the books and puts them in the cupboard, Moha wipes the blackboard and they all go out to the canteen.

She has to head home to have lunch, and though she looks longingly at the buoy from the car, she turns the ignition and leaves. There's nothing good on the radio at that time, but it's so close that she follows the intermittent line on the road and before she realises, she's already home.

Her flat has a little terrace where a small table and a couple of chairs fit, and she carries the reheated pasta, a glass of cold water, and a pomegranate outside. This pomegranate must have come from far away — perhaps from some greenhouse — because the season is beginning, but they're still green. Now that the heat isn't so oppressive, she likes having lunch on the little terrace, and in a few weeks she has developed a routine she fears she will have to adapt to the cold. Even in this mild climate winter will come.

It's three o'clock and she has the whole afternoon free. She could go back to the beach or go for a walk. Continue the book Dolors has lent her, take a nap. She could do whatever she likes, but she doesn't do anything. She remains seated on the terrace and watches how the afternoon advances, how the light changes.

The first night she spent alone in the flat she prepared to fill every minute: she called the children (as she would do every day) at eight, before they had dinner. They asked her how her day had gone and she laughed — *we spent most of it together, I've only been gone three or four hours!* She made herself dinner and watched a film, took some crosswords to bed. But she couldn't sleep and ended up on the terrace, listening to the waves, following the shadows of the bats. The terrace with two chairs. She put her feet up on the other one, more to occupy it than out of comfort.

When she had started to think about that first night, she had been afraid of feeling an enormous emptiness. She was surprised to experience the opposite. She found herself alone, not having to put anyone to bed, not having to think about whether she had prepared everything needed for their bags the following day, not having to decide with Paul whether to watch TV for a while or go to bed already. She didn't feel the terrible emptiness she was expecting. She felt only that she was, not having to do anything concrete for anyone else, she was there. And she realised she had missed herself the last few years.

'Miss, there's a book missing.'

'It'll have been Sneaky, she's in here for stealing.'

'If I smash your face in you'll run crying to the head, gayboy. At least I haven't been locked up for selling my ass.'

'Be a ho, don't say no. You've no choice but to steal because you're uglier than a dog.'

Sneaky threatens to break Salva's head, raises a chair. She asks Moha, who is usually calm, to go tell the supervisors. Salva, who is a head taller than Sneaky and has a muscular build, is on his feet, laughing at his classmate. Sneaky goes to hit him with the chair, but she gets between them.

She gets three stitches on her head and a considerable lump, Sneaky is punished with no weekend visits home for a month, and Salva is admonished for insulting her. 'They call me gayboy every day and here nothing happens, but I call out a thief and it blows up.' There is no point in arguing.

When she does the dead man's float that afternoon at the buoy, her injury stings. If it stings, it's healing, she tells the kids, as was often said to her. She's not in a hurry that afternoon, but the stitches are bothering her. She's not sure getting them wet was the right thing to do and is starting to feel cold. She goes back to the shore and gasps for breath: today, violence has robbed her of the sea. But just thinking this fills her with shame. Violence is robbing them of life. 'If it stings, it's healing' means something very different between the towering walls of the centre.

That night on the terrace, she looks at the few stars that can be seen above the light pollution of the tourist zone. She touches the bump and thinks about her children who like her to recite the names of the constellations.

'Miss, let's see the cut.'

'It's nothing, three little stitches. Also, I have so much hair you won't even see the scar.'

'Sneaky, you went too far.'

'When her husband comes looking for you, you're in the shit.'

'Miss, are you married?'

Deborah gives out the books. As one is missing, they now have to share in groups of three to look at it, but after the incident they are meeker, as if the outburst has relieved some tension and now they want to make it up to her somehow.

Using the book as an excuse some — those who come from elsewhere — speak of their own journeys. 'It's not like that, I didn't arrive on a big boat like that, I came on a plane.' 'When I arrived, everything seemed odd to me too, the food, the clothes, how people talked… Poor guy, he has to adapt.' Salma says nothing today either, and she doesn't ask her any questions. The girl will open up in time. Those from here describe their grandparents' journeys, longingly discussing lands that many of them have never seen. For her, feeling you are a stranger isn't only about migration. Feeling you are a stranger can be not reaching the buoy that calms you, not getting close enough to the sea. She says nothing, because once again she feels ashamed for thinking these things in front of the most marginalised of marginalised, before the young people kept apart so they don't pollute others, left to rot there, in an unassuming building in front of the sea that they almost never paddle in.

'I want to take the children on an outing.'

The head looks at her, unsurprised. Many new teachers have come to her office with the same request. They feel sorry for the children, want to save them. However, this is intriguing. They split her head open, and still she hasn't had enough.

'We could go to the park at the top of the nearby hill. It

will be exercise for them and I think it'll be good for the group dynamic. Roc and Dolors say they'll come with me.'

The head could say no, but really it's all the same to her. There's no-one too dangerous in the group, and it's unlikely they'll take the opportunity to escape. She doesn't yet know how complicated outings are, the newbie, and this way she'll learn. She'll make her do all the paperwork and wash her hands of it.

'Miss, can we play football? Roc brought the ball.'

The boys and a couple of girls assemble undersized teams, the other girls sit on a bench, she goes over to the lookout point. It's sunny, a little cool already, and the sea seems quiet and shining, a mirror splashed with purple. The towers of the hotels eat up the coast, and the aquatic park with its turquoise pools is an absurd imitation of the bright water so close by.

Salma comes over to her and leans on the iron handrail beside her. She looks at her for a moment and smiles. Both keep their eyes on the horizon.

'Miss, pardon. Book I, I have. I not wanted bad, I wanted read at night. I read very good in my house, my country. I read very good, good marks. Here not, here I not understand. I bring back book, say nothing.'

And she says nothing. She puts an arm around her shoulders, kisses the top of her head. She doesn't know if it's appropriate, she doesn't know if it's allowed, she doesn't know if she should do it. Salma moves away a little but doesn't leave. They continue to look at the sea. She touches the place where there had been a bump, which isn't there any longer; only the stitches, and they will soon fall out.

From afar Dolors looks at them and takes a photo. In the background, the sea.

CABARET

Everything you see now was kilos before. Kilos of soft, welcoming, smooth flesh. Kilos of pride achieved through force of will. Kilos of admirers asking where I am now, why I no longer perform, why I've abandoned them. Kilos of fat young women looking at me and feeling that yes, all the shit the troglodytes at school make them swallow is just that, shit, and the day will come when they'll be able to decide who to speak to and who not, and they'll only speak to those who look at them and see the beauty of their curves, the perfection of the fat under their taut skin.

I didn't want to be what I am now, all skin and bones, barely eighty kilos covering my skeleton. I woke up in hospital with a blurry memory of a vague discomfort, as if I was suddenly very tired, with a bad stomach, as if I'd eaten something that didn't go down well. 'You've had a heart attack,' said the doctor. 'You can't go on like this,' he said. This meant round, fat, perfect. This meant walking slowly but with style, happily taking up two seats on every plane, making the world uncomfortable with my undeniably present body.

It's strange, after struggling so much to be as I was, to find myself obliged to accept another body. Others, strangers, however, see me without noticing. I've disappeared, and a void that could end up being pleasant has surrounded me. I'm no longer looked at with disgust when I eat a doughnut in the street, or with pity when something falls on the ground and I have to bend down. I'm just another woman, a fifty-year-old woman like any other, not prettier or uglier or taller or shorter. Above all, not thinner or fatter. And a fifty-year-old woman who is nothing more than anyone else, simply isn't. In public, in the eyes of others, you know.

When I was fifteen, I'd have paid anything not to be. I'd have swallowed all my mother's pills if I'd known where she hid them. I'd have blown my head off with my father's gun if he'd had one.

I'd have drowned myself in the bathtub if it hadn't been so easy to keep breathing. And the more the not-being was denied to me, the more I was, the more I ate. Almost without wanting to, eating at odds with life.

I went putting on layers of fat to cover those I already had. It may seem a strange idea, hiding fat with more fat. But what if fat is really pain, and eating calms the pain and at the same time accumulates more fat that wants more food to be soothed?

Don't write that in the interview. Or maybe do, maybe it's worth writing. So people know it's been a painful road, that the success of the last twenty years didn't come from nowhere. So when a fat girl thinks she just isn't able anymore, she'll know she's not alone, that fifteen-year-old me is there beside her, not able anymore. So she'll realise that yes, she is able, life is stubborn and we cling to it even when it hurts to live.

Yes, these twenty years of success are what everyone knows. Me moving 135 kilos of comfort on the stage, me making jokes and pitying the poor skinnies who were less than a hundred kilos, me singing and dancing and laughing. Round, full of curves and complexities me, splendid and happy me, me imposing my body wherever I went. Me taking up all the space needed and more.

'You've had a heart attack,' said the doctor. 'You can't go on like this,' said the doctor. And life is such a fucker that we cling to it even when it demands we give up what we love most.

Before long I went onto the operating table knowing I'd come out the same on the outside but smaller inside, and this smallness would extend outwards. They'd make me a tiny stomach, I'd spend a month on a liquids-only diet, getting used to being less. Diet, exercise, diet. Learning to be less, losing layers, learning to lose the image I'd grown to want for myself.

After a year I'd lost almost half of my body and all meaning from my work. I left the stage, I completely disappeared. If I've agreed to see you today it's because of this girl and the letter she wrote me. Because one day she might wake up like me, in a hospital, before a doctor, and find herself obliged to choose between living or dying.

I won't lie, I'm finding it hard to disappear. But I've started walking on the beach every morning, with a mongrel I found abandoned and it seems he's been through the mill, too. Warm or cold, we go to the beach and we walk. I listen to the sea, as if it's saying my name, as if it sees me.

Everything you see now was kilos before. Kilos of protection, consolation, worry. Kilos of eating, wanting to fill a void. Everything you see now is the remains of a shipwreck I'm rebuilding into a boat, to sail overseas, joy within. Everything you see now is me, rediscovering myself, little by little.

VINCĖ — He had broad hands, like me, like my father. He had broad hands and when he came home and found me in the kitchen, he'd cover my eyes and ask me to guess who he was. 'Guess who?' seemed an innocent question, then. Just like when he was small, I'd keep up the ritual and ask him if he was his father, our neighbour, or the baker, and he'd laugh and say no. Just like when he was small, he'd laugh, with the newly-minted voice of a man, and from time to time still let out a squeak which always surprised him. 'It's Darius!' he'd shout as he hugged me and gave me a kiss, the few hairs emerging from his chin didn't scratch but always took me by surprise.

After a difficult labour, he was born small, and the fear of losing him still remained in my and Antanas' bodies. We had no more children, only him, and we raised him with the fear that he might break. Even when he was taller than me, he seemed a child, sitting in his corner, listening to the same tapes again and again, reading at times. He *was* a child, after all, who would often return from studying with some piece of wood. He was going to be a carpenter and build beautiful things with those broad hands that became rougher every day.

When I took him to the square as a little boy and he set off running after some scrawny cat, I'd bite my tongue so as not to shout at him. He had to grow up and become strong, chase cats as the rabble do, and if he fell, he had to learn to get back up. I couldn't always have him clinging to my skirts.

I also bit my tongue that night when he said he was going to defend parliament with his friends. My stomach turned as it had so many times while he was growing up, but I was treating him as grown-up and free, so I didn't tell him to wrap up warm, I didn't tell him to be careful, I didn't make any useless gestures. I stayed in the kitchen, finishing off the dishes, and reflected that there hadn't been sugar for days and there was hardly any flour left, and maybe the following day I'd send Darius to see what he could find on the other side of the city. I thought all this in the most unrealistic way, as if the following day might come, as if nothing was happening, while from the living room voices on the television could be heard saying there was a crowd of people on the streets looking to protect the parliament and the television tower. The unarmed people against the tanks. Nothing more than their stubborn presence against the tanks. How could this be?

I sat down beside my man in front of the television. At times they interrupted the broadcast with live images of the people in the streets and I futilely searched for Darius. We spent hours glued to the television, not speaking. Then the presenter, speaking to someone by telephone, said 'They're attacking us, I hear shots everywhere, I think they're coming.' She had a lovely hairstyle, and I thought I'd try it myself one of these days. After a while someone covered the camera and we saw nothing further. Antanas and I found ourselves watching the blankness left by the image on the screen when the signal cut out, and my stomach turned even more, like a knot or a stone, and I wanted to tell myself I was the same as ever, suffering for the little boy who almost died at birth, suffering because that labour was like chea-ting death and one day or another we would have to pay for it.

I opened the phone book and began calling his friends. That long night I dialled all the numbers I had and when it was early morning some answered. That long night I heard them say they hadn't seen anything, that they'd scattered with the first shots and lost sight of him.

I heard the fear in their voices, the nerves, and I didn't want to face up to the fact that they were lying. The hours passed and Darius didn't come home. There was talk of many wounded, and when we got to the television tower, we knew we would find him, we didn't say so but we knew, and we found him.

He'd been shot five times. In his legs, arms and back. Five

bullets in that body born so small, to which it had been so hard for me to give birth, now extinguished by five bullets. Arms meant to build beautiful things riddled with holes, broad hands with which he covered my eyes and asked me, like a child, guess who, now blood-soaked. One would have been enough; he'd never been strong, my Darius. But they shot him with five, five shots that kill me every day because I wanted to let him be grown-up and free, and I stayed silent when I needed to call him to his mother's side.

EURIKA — I took the words of the poet and gave them wings. I didn't know, that morning, that the people would come and I would give wind to those wings, that his words would become ours and would clothe us in what would be called the Singing Revolution.

I didn't know any way to revolt other than with song, and that's why that morning I took the words of the poet, swallowed them whole and let them come out, slowly, like a summer breeze, and fill the room. That's how the song was born, with no expectations. Just because sometimes words are not enough, the song was born.

Often, I'm asked how it feels when you go up on stage and see thousands of people applauding and screaming, people who know your songs. I don't know how to describe it; there's something strange about it. Time passes like a veil that polishes your memories and makes them malleable, and that's why I get to say that I've never felt on stage as I felt that day on the street, alongside all the others.

After so many hours shut inside, I'd gone out for some air. With no direction or aim beyond getting so far out of my head that I stopped thinking, I followed where my footsteps led me. I'd walked for an hour, maybe more, when I began to hear them. Thousands of voices, of all shades, all ages, all beauties. All were singing.

I crossed the street, followed the sound, and suddenly the

street opened up, exploding in my face. A crowd was holding hands and singing a song my grandmother had sung to me as a little girl. I went closer, a tall man smiled at me and offered me his hand, open-hearted like bread given to the hungry.

I sang with them. We sang. There were no recordings, no instruments, no programmes. When a song ended, someone must have just hummed another, and their neighbours must have followed, and the song spread like a wave. And then it began to sound familiar. Laisvė, freedom. My music, the poet's words, wind, wings.

I don't know now if it's the passing of time that made the tears run down my cheeks. I don't know if it's the passing of time that made my heart beat so hard it seemed to be breaking. I know I've never sung like I did that day, my voice happily inaudible among thousands of kindred voices.

When the song finished, before beginning the next, the man who had offered me his hand, the man whose arm I had grabbed as if it might have saved me from some ruthless precipice, looked at me. 'You sing very well,' he told me. And I smiled. 'Thank you,' I said.

EGLĖ — We were live but the phone rang, and it appeared I had to take it. It had been a while since the soldiers had taken our fellow editors; I'd seen it on the background monitor that was connected to the camera in the corridor. The cameraman nodded at me, more to bolster my spirits than to give me the permission I didn't need. I picked it up. The whole country was watching me. Everyone who wasn't on the street was glued to their television, and I was speaking. 'They're attacking us, I hear shots everywhere, I think they're coming.' The station director, Algirdas, asked me to continue broadcasting. And so I went on.

While our editor colleagues were here, those abroad were calling, and we knew more or less what to say. The tanks from the northern zone are approaching the city. They are armed.

The Soviet soldiers are charging the people. There are injuries. They've taken the telegraph office, the radio, they're coming this way.

And then we saw soldiers breaking down doors and taking colleagues away on the background monitor, and now it was only the cameraman and me live on air, and we no longer knew what to say — *We're here. We're trying to keep you informed. We're here.*

When they entered the studio, they seemed calm. 'Don't shoot, don't laugh, don't resist.' We didn't have weapons, but they thought we did. Someone covered the camera. I can't say I was afraid, perhaps because even though the barrel of the machine gun was sticking into my back it didn't seem as though they wanted to kill me. Or maybe I was just in a state of shock, and it only seemed I wasn't afraid.

It was worse when we went out onto the street. The night, the tanks, the soldiers, the screams. Collapsed walls, wounded people on the ground, soldiers beating those who weren't leaving, soldiers shooting at the unarmed crowd. People holding hands and praying. It was war, painfully dirty and real, war in my city. And me all eyes and ears and rage, etching all this in my mind, waiting for the moment to report.

The following day I found out that when the Soviets occupied the studio in Vilnius, my colleagues in Kaunas took over. They made a call to everyone who knew foreign languages to come onto the set, dozens of university professors turned up and began to broadcast in many languages, waiting for some station abroad to hear them.

The Swedish were the first to pay attention and explain it to the world. *We're here. We'll try to help you. We're here.*

GABRIELE — The winter was almost over and once the first few hours had passed at school, the air would warm up a little and we could take off our hats and scarves. The teacher gave the lesson with an energy that seemed normal to me at the time, but that I now find extraordinary. We were listening to her, doing our exercises, behaving ourselves. We'd adjusted rapidly to the new order of things, and it was as if we'd written in notebooks with our fingertips coming out of mittens all our lives.

Simas, who was sitting beside me, was drawing some lovely doves in the margins of his paper. I took off my glove and offered him the palm of my hand, and he drew me one that was flying, an olive branch in its beak.

At the end of the day, my mother was on the other side of the street waiting for me to go shopping for rice and some cans of food. In the adjoining neighbourhood everything was usually cheaper, and on the way we played at guessing what there would be that day, whether they'd have sugar, or if the coffee would already be gone. We weren't expecting the surprise, though: for the first time in months there was chocolate. More than the taste, I remember the excitement of going home, one hand holding my mother's hand, the little bar in the other, and deliberately dirtying my face, enjoying the pleasingly dense texture on my skin, too. I clutched the chocolate in the hand on which the hidden dove of peace was shining, with the branch in its beak.

We took the grand avenue. No cars had circulated there for a long time as no-one had petrol or knew where to get any; there was a strange beauty in that enormous space, devoid of sound. Since that January night, I couldn't hear too well in my right ear, and I was relaxed by the silence that didn't require you to listen to anything. On television they discussed it a lot, the tanks attacking the television tower, but at home we limited ourselves to replacing the broken glass and making out as if we hadn't had the tanks there at all, as if we hadn't lived through the fear of projectiles tearing the night, as if my ear hadn't been burst and left me with an insistent ringing for so many days, a ringing that still comes back at times, even now.

Mother, of course, heard the commotion before me and

looked back, surprised. After a short while I could hear it too: festival music. It came closer, down the avenue towards us, growing ever stronger, until the first musicians of the band began to appear, and after them the dancers, and after them a flame-breathing fakir, a clown with a monkey, a magician in a top hat.

People stood still on the pavements to let the entourage past which was coming to announce the circus. The great deserted avenue filled with marvelling glances, children pointing at the musicians and clowns, adults with shining eyes.

I wasn't taken to see the circus that week at the end of winter. But, linked to the dense flavour of chocolate, I'll for evermore recall that day in the centre of Vilnius when I saw an enormous white elephant closing the parade of circus artistes.